Anke Bär

Wilhelm's Journey

An Emigration Story

North
South

For my grandmother
and for Christian,
who both set forth on the most
unimaginable journey of all.
—A.B.

 GOETHE INSTITUT The translation of this work was supported by a grant from the Goethe-Institut in the framework of the *Books First* program.

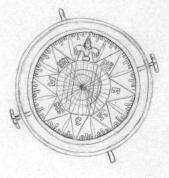

First published in the United States, Great Britain, Canada, Australia, and New Zealand in 2019 by NorthSouth Books, Inc., an imprint of NordSüd Verlag AG, CH-8050 Zürich, Switzerland.
Distributed in the United States by NorthSouth Books, Inc., New York 10016.
Library of Congress Cataloging-in-Publication Data is available.

ISBN: 978-0-7358-4352-3 (trade edition)
1 3 5 7 9 · 10 8 6 4 2
Printed in Latvia by Livonia Print, Riga, 2019.
www.northsouth.com

MIX
Paper from
responsible sources
FSC® C002795

North
South

Table of Contents

Grandma Days

Anna's grandmother had old family photos on her wall. Anna liked to look at the pictures. She especially liked the photo of a boy with a hat that looked like a baseball cap. The little boy seemed somehow familiar to her, while the other stern-looking "ancestors" scared her a bit. Wilhelm, the boy in the photo, didn't know that one day he would be Anna's great-great-grandpa.

Anna's grandma was a great keeper of old family stories and wonderful objects. She had whole collections of them—in her head and on the shelves. Oh, yes! Grandma liked to tell tales from long ago. Many of her stories were about Wilhelm. Anna couldn't get enough of hearing about his adventurous life.

One day, wearing a mysterious expression, her grandma took out an old, yellowed notebook. "If you're very careful, you can look at it," she said. Anna started to turn the pages and suddenly found herself in a time long ago. It felt as if Wilhelm was talking to her.

150 Years Ago

Iwas born in 1857. My family and I lived in a single room—a farmer's hut—in a village in the Spessart Mountains. I'm lucky to be alive! I was delivered on a moldy straw bed. It was all we had. There was no doctor to make sure it all turned out okay. Mom says Dad knelt next to the bed with folded hands to thank God that she and I had made it.

The other peasant kids and I work on the farm all day. It's so tiring. I'd love to have a big, warm meal to eat, but we'll go to bed hungry again tonight. I can hear my brother's stomach growling. I rarely get to go to school, since Dad needs help on the farm. Dad says working on the farm comes first. My parents say, "Reading and writing are fine, but they won't help plow a field." On the days I do get to go, our school doesn't even have any books or pencils. The only book in our whole house is the *Bible*. If you're wondering how I'm writing this now, it's only because a great man taught me to read and write. I'll tell you about that next. It all started when Grandpa gave me a carving knife. Woodcarving is my favorite thing to do when I'm not working on the farm or going to school.

What luck! I have just turned twelve, and there is a woodcarving school in the neighboring village where kids from poor families like mine can get an education. You don't have to pay any money for an apprenticeship; you get three meals a day, and you even sleep in a real bed! I hope Dad lets me go. I've carved more than twenty wooden figures so far.

J talked to Dad, and he didn't want to lose my help at home, but he finally gave in and registered me at the woodcarving school. I made a new friend: Georg, the workshop manager. The work each day is exhausting, but every night, Georg helped me practice reading and writing. I spent many hours a day for three years drawing and sculpting there. That's how I can write this. Now I read very well. I read everything that passes my eyes. One day, I saw a newspaper report on American emigrants. They say in America you can get farmland for free—as a gift—after being there five years. The people in my village say that in America, all—really all—people are happy and content, and you can find fist-size pieces of gold and live without a care for the rest of your entire life. America! What's keeping me in this little village?

An America-recruiter has come to the area. He disappeared into the house of the mayor. It's been decided: an expedition of emigrants will be formed from the surrounding villages—including ours.

The news spread like wildfire. I ran straight to the mayor without thinking twice and asked for admission to the trek even before I talked to Dad about it. Dad doesn't want me to go. He seems annoyed that I asked, but he finally gave in—just like with the woodcarving school. Together he and I entered my name to the list of applicants.

Farewell to the Mountains

At last, the great day has finally come: the journey is going to begin! I ran one last time through the rain-soaked lanes of our village, bidding farewell. A pig grunted in the mud. I heard the chirping of the blackbirds and the familiar rippling of the brook. I plucked a leaf from the village lime tree, dropped it into the water, and watched as it was carried away. Perhaps it would still reach the sea before me . . .

I made my way across the open fields to the neighboring village to say good-bye to the woodcarving school and to my friend Georg, the workshop manager. He gave me a real treasure, this sketchbook! Here is what Georg wrote in copperplate:

Get to know the world through your drawings. I will miss you. Your teacher Georg 1872

Departure for Foreign Lands

I got up early the next morning to join the emigrants' trek. I could still see the moon in the sky! My parents looked so small as they watched from the cottage. My brothers and sisters waved and wiped their eyes. Why were they crying? They think I might not come back. What if they're right? I was about to return to my family, but then I heard the whistle blow. It was now or never. I ran toward the ship and my new life.

I never would have been able to raise the money for a trip to America myself. A relief fund for the poor helped: money was collected, as it was in other villages, to let people like me—the poorest of the poor—go on the voyage. In my village, there was nowhere to work, and I didn't have the money to start my own workshop. But I didn't let that make me feel sad, like some of the other people who were gathered to go. I couldn't wait to see the world beyond the village. I ran ahead of our small group.

WHY DID EMIGRANTS LEAVE THEIR HOMELAND?

Not only in the Spessart Mountains, but other regions of Germany were also hopelessly overpopulated in the nineteenth century. There was not enough farmland for the many farmers' families. And then there were no other job opportunities. Industrialization had been introduced in Germany. Small workshops and manufacturers were replaced by large factories, with their machines and cheap labor. Weavers and spoon-makers, blacksmiths and shoemakers hoped for work opportunities in distant America. And those who had only a little bit of land in their home country, or had worked as a servant, dreamed of founding a large farm in the New World as a settler.

But not only pressing poverty and the prospect of a better income in America prompted men and women throughout Europe to give up their current lives and cross the Atlantic. Some left for religious or political reasons. Some were persecuted and fled to avoid prison or death. Others did not have to worry about their lives, but they did not want to be kept in the yoke of an unjust ruler.

The pilgrims were deemed to be the first European settlers of America. They crossed the Atlantic on the famous Mayflower in 1620.

Overland

This was the first time I left the area where I grew up. Farmers who lived in poverty, like my family, never had vacations, not even days off. Only Sundays with visits to the church were different from the constant sameness of our days.

It took many days for our journey to Bremerhaven. We walked a long time; then took a train.

Cars had not been invented yet. Horse-drawn carriages were the main means of transport.

My feet are hurting!

Some say, "The trains run so slowly that you can pick flowers during the journey."

That's okay with me as long as I don't have to walk!

Steaming Monstrosity

At the Port

There she is—the *Columbia*—the ship that's going to take us across the Atlantic. It's in the old part of the harbor, away from the busy ocean liners. Her masts stretch majestically into the sky. It's a cool morning, and a misty veil hangs over the harbor basin. Up in the rigging of the ship, sailors are busy preparing for the departure. Their shouts are ringing out back and forth.

As I look over the water toward the open sea, the expanse is overwhelming. The wind here is nothing like the wind in the Spessart Mountains: it tastes salty and ruffles my hair. Above the masts, large white birds are fighting with loud shrieks over a newly caught fish.

My traveling companions from the Spessart Mountains are gone! They disappeared into the crowd. I feel lonely even though I'm in the midst of all these people waiting to climb aboard the *Columbia*. I can't understand a word anyone around me is saying. They are talking in foreign languages and unknown dialects.

Hafenansicht
Bremerhaven 1865

The Columbia

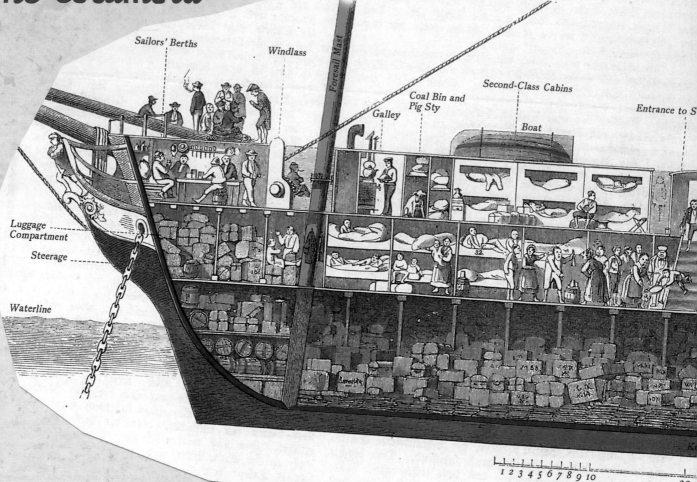

Sailors' Berths   Windlass   Foresail Mast   Galley   Coal Bin and Pig Sty   Second-Class Cabins   Boat   Entrance to S

Luggage Compartment

Steerage

Waterline

1 2 3 4 5 6 7 8 9 10   20

Finally everybody has found a place in one of the five-bed bunks that have been hammered into steerage in upper and lower rows for our journey to America. Gradually, the knot of people, crates, and boxes unties itself.

Everyone has been pushing to get onto the ship and rushing to find a good place. In the half-dusk of steerage, I stumbled over trunks and bundles, ducked under menacing fists, and did my best to avoid loud arguments. I was looking for familiar faces.

And indeed, I finally met again some companions from the Spessart Mountains, and even found a free bunk place in their vicinity. I share the bunk with four giants who don't understand a word of German.

Mainmast

Foremast

Square Sail

Mizzenmast

Staysail

Bowsprit and Jibboom

16

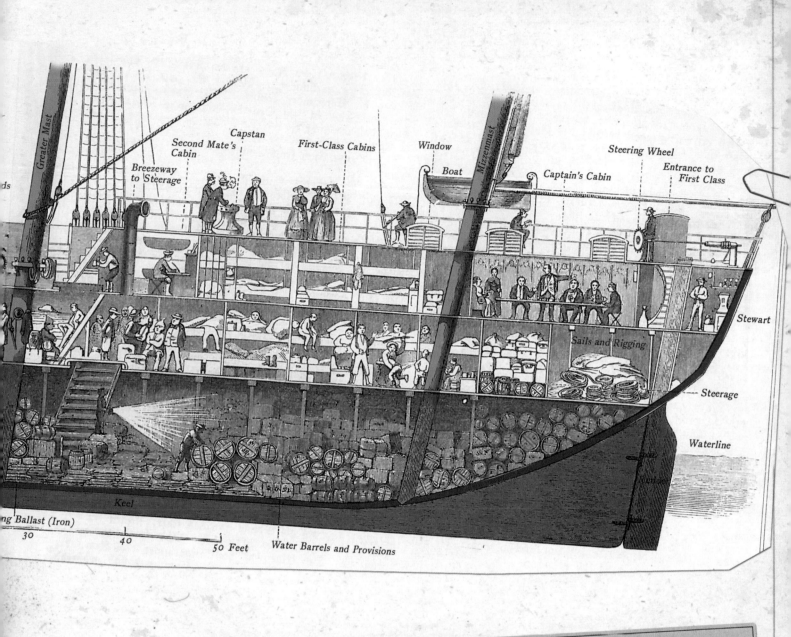

Greater Mast

Breezeway to Steerage

Second Mate's Cabin

Capstan

First-Class Cabins

Window

Boat

Mizzenmast

Captain's Cabin

Steering Wheel

Entrance to First Class

Stewart

Sails and Rigging

Steerage

Waterline

Water Barrels and Provisions

Keel

Ballast (Iron)

30   40   50 Feet

Zwischendeck

Nach Amerika von BREMEN nach Newyork Baltimore Neworleans

Auswanderungswillige! Braucht ihr Rat u. Auskunft über Auswanderungsmöglichkeiten (Reisegelegenheit, Verhältniffe im Ausland u. a.)?

As Far As the Eye Can See

It's the first morning on the open sea! I woke when some children ran screaming through steerage. I hurried to get dressed and followed them up the steep staircase and through the hatch to the fresh air. We had to squint because of the bright morning sun after the darkness of steerage. The sea is quiet. All around nothing but water–all the way to the horizon . . . Above stretches a blue sky, interspersed by small clouds that look like a herd of fabulous beings. A few terns circle the masts of the ship. The sails snap in the wind.

Seasick

As the day wears on, my enthusiasm for life on the high seas has waned. Seasickness has hit me with full force as well as more than half of the approximately four hundred passengers.

Nausea

Seasickness is a mysterious, unpredictable condition. Most scientists believe that it occurs because the brain is confused by contradictory information from the sensory organs. The swell of the sea and the constantly changing position of the ship in the water make the eyes perceive impressions different from those received by the organs of equilibrium.

Most people get used to the movements of the ship after a while, and the symptoms of seasickness and nausea gradually diminish. But the complaints can also last very long. In the most drastic cases of seasickness, passengers must be tied down so that they do not hurl themselves overboard. At least today there are some drugs known to alleviate somewhat the nausea.

Rum and Castor Oil

Fortunately, my seasickness abated after a few days, but all around are fellow travelers plagued by nausea. Vomit, overturned chamber pots, clothes stiff with dirt, and unwashed bodies spread a terrible stench in the confines of steerage. Everything is clammy, and the constant moisture encourages mold. Bedbugs and other vermin have crawled through the bunks, plaguing us all with their bites and stings.

Sick at Sea

There was no real doctor on an emigration ship until the end of the nineteenth century. As a rule, the captain acted as pharmacist, but one that was not very familiar with the treatment of illnesses. He used a simple leaflet listing various symptoms and illnesses, and prescribed medicine from cross-referenced, numbered vials from the pharmacy.

On the emigration ships from Bremerhaven to America, deaths were relatively rare because hygienic conditions were quite tolerable compared to the situation on other emigration ships. Diseases, however, could spread easily in the narrow confines of steerage.

Fleabites

Mustard Oil
of Herbs
barb

Faint	Valerian
	Hoffmann's Elixir of Life
Inflammation	Chamomile Oil
Fever	Hydrochloric Quinine
Constipation	Castor Oil
	Epsom Salt
Scurvy	Lemon Juice
Wounds	Theden's Wound Water
	Rubber Bandages
Bleeding	Drops of Cinnemon Oil
Cramps	Amber Hartshorn
Choking Attacks	Sulfuric Gold

Hidden Passengers

Bedbug bites everywhere! Where one bedbug appears soon there will be a multitude.

The lice comb is being used all the time.

Lice

Bedbugs

Fleas

There is no one on board who does not constantly scratch.

Roaches

Previously killed cockroaches: 27! Harmless, but disgusting. Sometimes as long as a whole thumb.

The passengers slept closely together and so the fleas, bedbugs, and lice could easily migrate from one person to the other and spread diseases.

At that time people did not know so much about the body and the treatment of diseases as today.

Scabies Mites

Pastime

I enjoy watching the people on board, trying to guess who they are, where they want to go, and what is going on with them. I draw tirelessly in my sketchbook. The leather cover is becoming tanned by salt water, wind, and sun.

I'm beginning to know many of my fellow travelers, just as Georg predicted. And they are beginning to know and trust me as I sit bent over my sketchbook, taking notes, observing, and drawing. I hear them say: "Over there he sits again, scribbling and dreaming—the scribbling Johnny!"

A while ago I whistled
a little song, and a sailor
came to me horror-struck:
"You are whistling up
a storm!"

Daily Routine
of the
Steerage Passengers

0600 hours Getting up
and washing
(sleeping longer
is impossible)
Mealtimes (approximate):
0800 hours - Breakfast
1300 hours - Midday Meal
1800 hours - Supper

Hardtack and Preserved Meat

Even during meals you can meet all sorts of creatures. I learned from the sailors that it's advisable to tap the ship's hardtack before soaking it in soup. A few maggots always tumble out from within the bread. I am grateful for the food we have on board. I remember very well how it felt going to bed with a growling stomach. I never complain about the stews and soups that are always the same, about pickled, overly salted meat, and sauerkraut boiled into oblivion or mashed potatoes boiled into pulp. I only wonder how the ship's chief cook manages to prepare food for several hundred people in the small galley.

Fresh Fish

NUTRITION ON BOARD

The Columbia *had loaded provisions for ninety days at sea, although in good-weather conditions the passage usually lasted only about six weeks.*

This stockpile was a requirement since the course of a sailing vessel was never exactly predictable. It was redefined day by day depending on wind direction and wind force. Torrential storms could drive the ship far off course, and doldrums sometimes hindered progress for days.

Potable water also had to be carried along on board. The hold of the Columbia *held a huge tank. Storage of drinking water for a long time was difficult at that time because it became stagnant easily. Therefore a favorite drink among sailors was grog: water with a dash of rum for disinfecting and for the taste; sometimes sugar and lemon juice were also added. For the passengers there was mainly weak coffee or tea.*

Live Provisions

Sauerkraut

Potatoes

Apples

Grain

Brined Meat

Vegetables Suitable for Storage

Pudding in a Cloth

Peas

Beans

Lentils

CAPTAIN'S PRIVILEGE
The captain and the
officers were entitled
to live provisions and
freshly caught fish
first.

RECIPE:
EMIGRANTS' SUNDAY PUDDING

2 cups flour
1 cup chopped kidney fat or beef tallow
(or butter—for those who can afford it)
possibly some sugar
possibly some water

Knead the ingredients into a supple dough that
no longer sticks to the fingers. Roll it out about the
thickness of a knife. Then place the dough on a pudding
cloth or dish towel that has been well rubbed with fat
and sprinkled with flour. If there is some, smear the
dough with jam. Roll it up carefully and cover it with
the cloth. Tie the two open ends carefully together.
Hang this on a stick placed across the rim of a pot
of boiling water and make sure that the towel does
not touch bottom. Cook evenly for about two hours.

Hardtack

Soup

Grain Porridge

Stews

Bucket and Bilge

Until way into the eighteenth century, sailors tried to improve the cloying air in steerage with smoking juniper branches, tobacco, and sulfur.

In order to do our business, the other steerage travelers and I use a simple bucket. Using the bucket isn't so easy, especially for women, who usually wear several layers of heavy clothes and underskirts. I'm plagued by hard constipation because there is no place to do my business that is private. After use, the contents of the bucket has to be tipped overboard and then the bucket is let down into the water by a long rope for cleaning. The sailors often use the jibboom net as a toilet. It's said that there is a sort of water closet with a recessed bucket at the disposal of the first-class passengers, the captain, and the officers. But during storms, all of them regardless of rank or class have to use a chamber pot or go somewhere belowdecks.

Underwear or underpants were called the "unmentionables" but were not commonly in use.

The perforated toilet paper roll — as we know it — was not invented until the late nineteenth century.

BILGE

The unappetizing soup that accumulated at the very bottom of the ship was a brew of water, excrement and urine, rotten waste, and rats' poop: the so-called bilge. From time to time the bilge was pumped out in order to reduce the risk of disease on board.

WASHING SODA

Salt water reduces the cleaning power of soap. Washing soda helped. But the garments, washed in salt water, became stiff and sticky, and felt unpleasant on the skin, so some would not wash their clothes at all.

VENTILATION OF THE LOWER DECKS

Ventilation of the lower decks was very poor because where no water could penetrate, no air could either. From time to time sailors tried to draw fresh air into the ship's hold with tubes of canvas.

BATHING LADDER

At that time many people could not swim at all. Besides, little was known about the world under the water's surface. Who would guarantee that there were not huge sea monsters lurking in the deep, waiting to devour the bathers? Swimming in the sea was hardly ever possible, if at all, and then only during very calm weather.

Joy and Suffering

I spend most of the time drawing. My sketchbook is my best friend and helps keep away the boredom. But at night a great loneliness creeps in. I lay awake, squeezed between snoring giants who roll over onto me and puff into my ears. I long for my little sister, Mimi, who I slept next to at home in the Spessart Mountains.

Tonight we were in the middle of a huge thunderstorm! The muffled crashing of thunder and the roar of the storm made us feel like our world was on the brink of destruction. I conjured up comforting images from home: the cow, Lieselotte, and the little house by the stream, the face of my mother or of Georg carving wood in the workshop. The travelers around me squeezed their hands together in prayer in the musty darkness of steerage and pleaded with God for mercy. I heard them whispering all around me.

But the storm has passed! After surviving the roar and rage of the thunderstorm, people are happily celebrating and dancing, playing music and singing on board the *Columbia*. The separation between steerage and cabin passengers, between captain, crew, and emigrants seems temporarily suspended. The children are playing pranks, hiding behind broad backs and between long skirts. I sit quietly and record it all in my journal.

LIVING TOGETHER IN A CONFINED SPACE

For the time of the crossing, several hundred people had to get along with one another in a very small space. As in each group, there were also leaders on the Columbia who took care of many problems. There were those who easily flew off the handle and those who calmed things down, inconspicuous ones and birds of paradise, worrywarts and optimists. The people laughed, quarreled, lamented loudly or suffered quietly, were silent and withdrawn or sociable and communicative. Some saw each other again and again, first in glances, then in talks, and then to the forging of common plans for America. Even a wedding was celebrated on the Columbia and several engagements on top and, of course, birthdays. A girl got to know her future employer on board. A traveler who spoke English well offered free lessons on some days. And some who suffered particularly from idleness and boredom came to the sailors' aid and helped, for example, with the patching of the sails.

Favorite Games

The children look curiously over my shoulder as I draw. Once I find a good place to sit, I pull out my sketchbook, set out my pens, and it isn't five minutes before I am surrounded by a bunch of children who eagerly talk to me.

The children like to follow the sailors.

CHILDREN ON BOARD

The children of steerage passengers had few or no toys at all. And if so, they were almost always homemade: carved wooden figures, simple dolls made of rags, or round pebbles stored in a small cloth bag. Clay marbles were an exquisite treasure.

There are plenty of ropes and cordage.

PLAYING WITHOUT TOYS

Actually, you do not need much to play with other children. To play catch, hide-and-seek, tussling, singing, solving riddles, inventing stories—all of this is free. And you always have yourself—your body as a "toy" and your imagination. This makes it possible to invent new games all the time, and the children on board the Columbia did just that.

Button, Button, Who's Got the Button?

I feel closer to the children on the *Columbia* than to the adults. Sometimes I join a group of children who are listening to a fairy tale, or I join their hide-and-seek games and play catch with them, or put little boys on my shoulders to fight battles, or collect leftover pieces of wood from the ship's carpenter from which some children and I fashion figures or small ships. On deck I can often hear the sounds of the children laughing, shrieking, and singing against the snapping of the sails and the whistling of the wind, wording rhymes, or telling one another riddles. The children have invented a new game. They use the swaying of the ship to let themselves fall together in a heap, or have competitions to see who can keep his or her balance the longest—on one leg or even in a handstand.

THE GOLDEN BRIDGE

Golden, golden, bridge, who broke the bridge? The

goldschmith, the goldschmith, with h -is youngest daughter. Pass

all through, pass all through. We want to catch the last one, with

spe- ars and with st- icks!

Wolf

Duck

I can only live
where there is light,
but I die if light
shines on me.
What am I?

Favorite Games on Board:
Games of Forfeit or
Showdown
(TUG-OF-WAR, ARM WRESTLING,
THUMB WRESTLING)
also Hide-and-Seek
and Cat's Cradle!

THE GOLDEN BRIDGE: GAME INSTRUCTIONS

Two children take hold of each other's hands and form a bridge through which the remaining children walk continuously, over and over. With the last note of the song, the arms snap down and catch the child who is there. The child now has to decide which side he or she wants to join. The song is repeated until all the children are on either side of the bridge.

The two gatekeepers previously decided in secret who is from heaven and who is from hell. At the end, all the children who are on the heaven side are gently rocked on crossed arms:

Angel, angel, you are heavy with gold and silver!
High up in the sky and down to Earth.

Then it is the hell children's turn, and they are pushed one after the other between the arms of the gatekeepers:

Who screams and screeches in my house?
The devil! We chase him out the gate!

Take off my skin
and I won't cry,
but you will.
What am I?

Day and Night

The *Columbia* has fallen into a state of the doldrums, and it's lasted for several days. We don't seem to be moving forward. The sluggish roll of the ship and the daily monotony on board is making people irritable. The tone between the sailors is becoming more aggressive, and there is constant quarreling in steerage.

Now, abruptly, the weather has changed! The listlessly flapping sails have filled again with the rising wind. The breeze on my sunburned skin and sweaty hair feels refreshing. Everywhere around me, people are laughing with relief and holding up their fluttering handkerchiefs.

During a storm linens were stretched across important places on the deck.

The sailors could then walk along hand-over-hand or tie themselves to it in order not to fall overboard.

FROM BREMERHAVEN TO NEW YORK

The Columbia, *coming from the North Sea, crossed the English Channel and sailed south, along the coastlines of France, Spain, and Portugal, and farther along the African coast. She passed the Canary Islands, sailed westward with the trade winds near the Cape Verde Islands.*

The captain followed the traditional route for crossing the Atlantic. He circumnavigated areas where the ship could experience doldrums and tried to use favorable wind conditions. Even so, the crew of the Columbia *had to contend with dangerous waters and violent storms. Torn sails and burst wood resulted in several tedious repairs.*

We are sinking in our own muck. The storms are raging so that the stairs have been closed for days. The chamber pots are overflowing and often tip over in the violent waves.

Nautical Science

Despite our route along the coasts, the mainland is usually not visible from the ship. The captain takes measurements on the quarterdeck. I've been hanging around at the foot of the stairs for days, because I would have loved to look closely at or even draw the strange devices that he used, but the steerage passengers are not permitted to step on the quarterdeck. Yesterday the captain actually waved me up and asked to take a look at my sketchbook. My drawings seem to have impressed him.

Chip Log *Zero Mark* *1st Knot* *2nd Knot*

THE CHIP LOG

The chip log measures the speed of the ship in knots. For this the captain or an officer lets the log into the water and counts how many knots run through his hand until the sand has drifted through the log glass (a special type of hourglass). Indicating speed in knots is still used today in the shipping industry.

CELESTIAL NAVIGATION

For many centuries seafarers had been able to determine the geographical latitude on which a ship was actually located by means of celestial altitude. This meant that during an Atlantic crossing, they knew that they would reach their destination if they sailed to the east or west (depending on the destination) along the desired latitude. But it was not until the middle of the eighteenth century that instruments could determine the longitude. These instruments used for angle measurements—the octant, sextant, and chronometer—were invented and used with the nautical almanac, which listed the exact celestial positions of the stars. With complicated measures and calculations, destinations could be approached much more precisely. Before that time, only hourglasses were available.

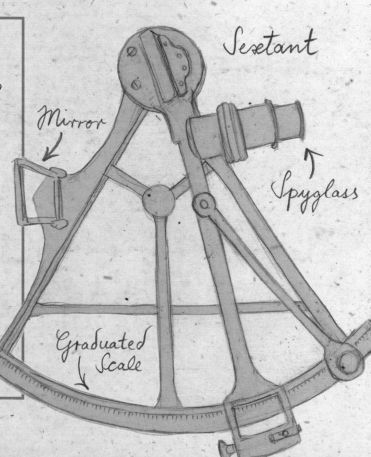

Sextant

Mirror

Spyglass

Graduated Scale

Chip Log

The thread suspension of the magnetic needle is clearly visible.

Stowed in the binnacle

Magnetic Compass

The chronometer is a very accurate ship clock This is certainly very valuable.

Marine Chronometer

THE MAGNETIC COMPASS

On the large sailing ships, the navigator used a binnacle placed on the center line of the ship. A lubber line on the binnacle showed him the actual course of the ship.

On board a large sailing ship such as the Columbia there were other compasses: bearing compasses (to determine the direction of an object, for example, a beacon) and reserve compasses.

The Route

The captain showed me the art prints that adorn
the walls of his cabin! On the table, a large marine
chart was spread out on which the route of the
Columbia is recorded. Next to it are sheets of paper
covered with long columns of numbers. I looked as
closely as I could in the half-dark room.

Books were arranged along the wall. The captain smiled at me and
laid a few thick volumes on the table. I leafed through them and
was totally astonished. Whole worlds of sea monsters and
marine gods, figureheads and famous sailing ships, fish
and other marine life spread out before my eyes.

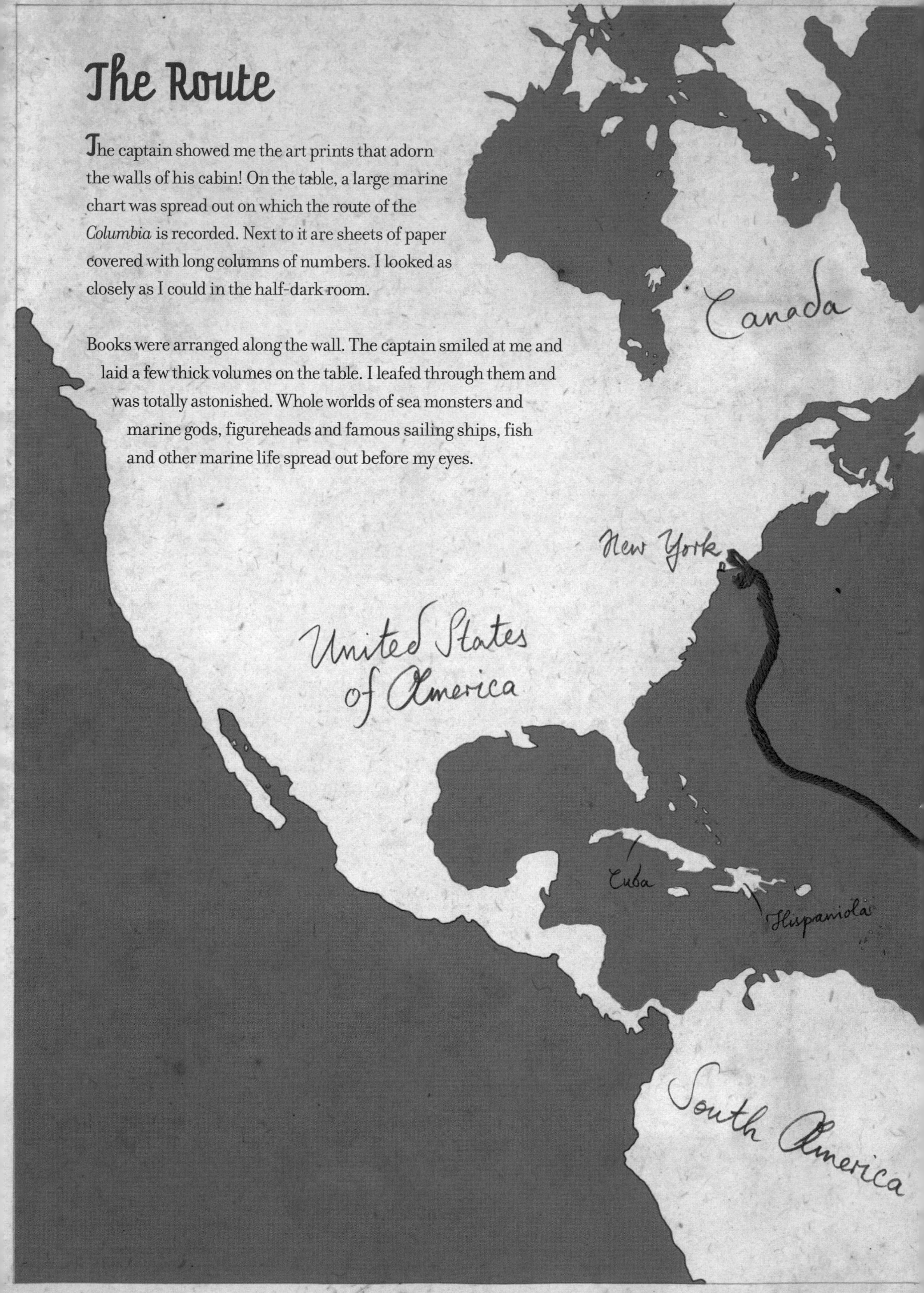

Canada

New York

United States
of America

Cuba

Hispaniola

South America

Greenland

Iceland

Scandinavia

Newfoundland

Bremerhaven

Europe

The red thread marks
in a very simplified way
the zigzag course of the
Columbia, which could
not follow such an
ideal route because of
her dependence on
prevailing winds.

Canary
Islands

Africa

Ravenous Sea

I'm beginning to know some of the sailors. I particularly like Arend, the boatswain. In order to work at sea, you cannot be scared by the idea of losing your life from one day to the next. Arend told me a lot about the faith of many sailors, who believe that the souls of those swallowed by the sea continue to live in seagulls, albatrosses, and petrels.

FIGUREHEADS

Figureheads are the wooden carved figures that were affixed under the bowsprit of many great sailing ships. The sailors believed that they would point the ships the right way and protect them from misfortune. If a figurehead was damaged or even lost, the sailors expected really bad luck.

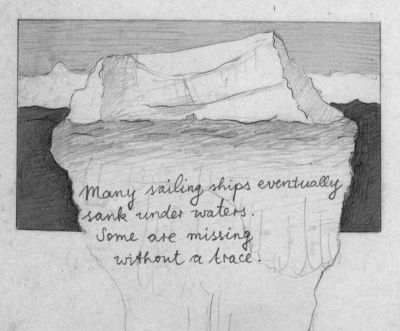

Many sailing ships eventually sank under waters.
Some are missing without a trace.

ICEBERGS

Floating icebergs are dangerous to ships because they protrude only about one-seventh out of the water. By the time you see an iceberg, the collision is often already imminent.

At the bottom of the oceans lie thousands of sunken ships, some laden with treasures that are lost forever.

Animal Companions

Large, elegant fish often swim alongside the *Columbia*. Sometimes they keep near the side, sometimes near the front of the ship. I never get bored watching them. A teacher told us that they are dolphins, which do not belong to the fish classification but rather are mammals because they give birth to live young.

A small flying fish landed on the deck just before my feet. A fish with wings! It could not swim out of my hand, so I got to marvel at him for a while.

Terns

Flying Fish

Nurse Shark

Sea Bream

Porpoise

Hammerhead Shark

Swordfish

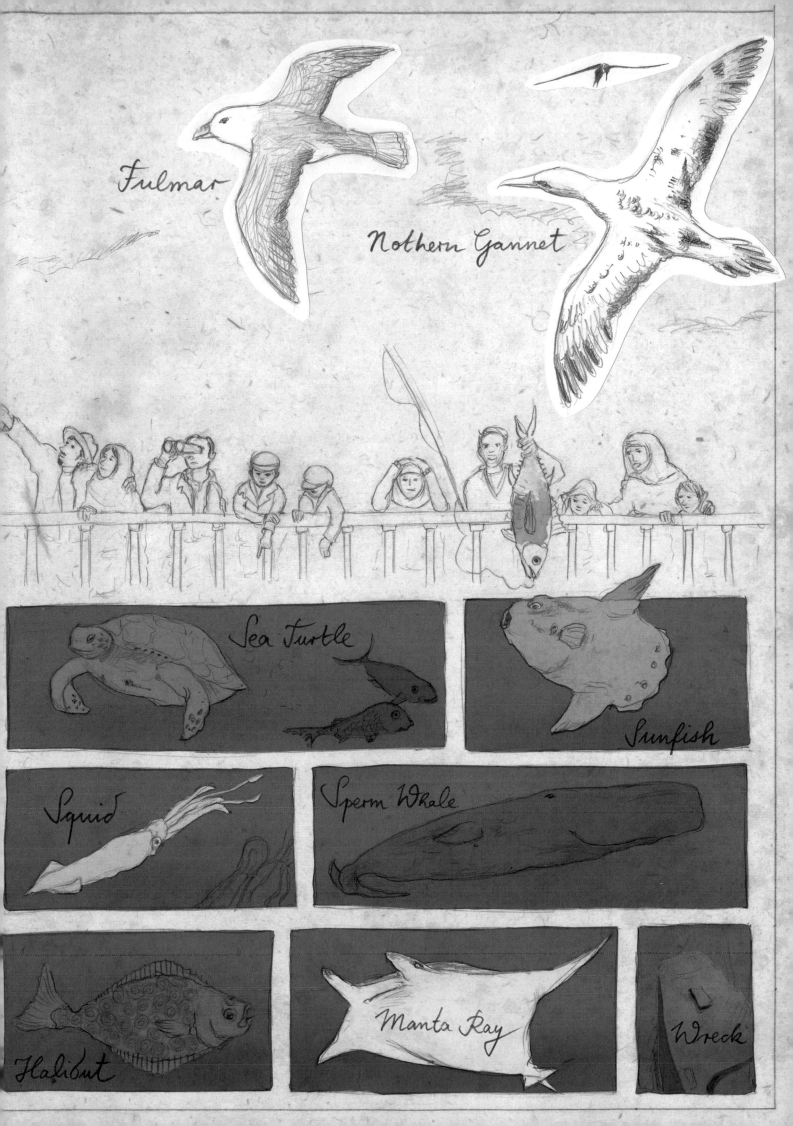

Secrets at Night

One night I awoke because I really had to go. I used the chamber pot because the travelers are not supposed to leave steerage at night. But the stink around me took my breath away; I thought I was suffocating and ran to the exit.

Up on the deck, I leaned against the railing, relieved, and drew the cool night air deeply into my lungs. When I looked at the waves, I could not believe my eyes: the sea luminesced! A green glow was everywhere on the crests of the waves. The hull of the *Columbia* was surrounded by phosphorescent luminescent spots. It looked eerie and beautiful at the same time. I almost thought I saw the green hair and scaly tails of mermaids among the glittering waves.

For the sailors on watch, it seemed that this wasn't their first time seeing the luminescing sea, because they continued with their work, unfazed by the dramatic light show.

MARINE PHOSPHORESCENCE

Sometimes the sea shines because millions of microorganisms are stimulated by touch to emit their light. Dinoflagellates, a type of algae, are often responsible for marine phosphorescence, but there are other marine dwellers that luminesce—for example, lantern fish and pyrosomes.

MERMAIDS

In the nineteenth century, many people still believed in the existence of mermaids. There were museums that exhibited supposedly true mermaid mummies and skeletons: mostly small, wizened, ugly figures. In reality, however, the exhibits were made by crooks who earned a lot of money from them.

When dolphins sleep, one half of their brain always remains awake. One eye even remains open.

Life at Sea

J enjoy the nightly calm of the abandoned deck. I sneak out more frequently these days when I cannot sleep. On the second night I met Arend, the boatswain whom I had befriended. Arend too enjoyed the peace on deck.

Arend told me of life at sea—on a few square feet but surrounded by the vast expanse of the ocean—and that this infinity sometimes frightened him, of the never-ending journey and the longing for home, of the common struggle of the sailors with the forces of nature, and that it was not possible to avoid each other after a fight. The life of the sailors followed its own rules and laws, and it had little in common with the lives of the people on the mainland.

Sailmaker

First Mate

Second Mate

Captain

Cabin Boy

Ship's Carpenter

The Crew

The crew of the Columbia included twenty-four sailors: captain, first mate and second mate, boatswain, ship's carpenter, chief cook, sailmaker, seven sailors, four ordinary seamen (sailors in training), and four cabin boys. The work on board was controlled by a so-called two-watch system. A watch included six hours, or in the seamen's language twelve bells. The term "bell" comes from the fact that before the invention of the chronometer, time was actually measured with an hourglass—the sandglass—that had to be turned over every half hour. At the same time, the ship's bell was rung and the time was given by the number of rings of the bell. If danger threatened and the command "All hands on deck!" sounded, a free watch (free time) could be interrupted rudely.

Chief Cook

Boatswain
(responsible for ropes, sails, and anchors)

Several Thousand Yards of Rope

When the weather is good, I take a nap on the deck after lunch. Lying flat on my back, I let my eyes climb up the masts and sails until I lose myself between the countless ropes that stretch in all possible directions, hanging down loosely or entwined. It's a mystery to me, how the sailors can tell all the ropes apart.

Arend told me that several thousand yards of rope are used on the *Columbia*. He also taught me the most important seaman's knots and a few English chanteys.

How to turn a cord:

Twist two or more threads together.

Fig. 1

Weigh down with scissors or something similar.

Fig. 2

HEAVY ROPES (REEP LANES, OR "REEPERBAHNEN")

According to the same principle as that of turning a cord, ropes for ships (reeps) were made on "reep lanes" (Reeperbahnen). The rope makers (or reep beaters)—the craftsmen who made the ropes—turned the ropes in lanes up to sixty yards long. Hemp was mostly used because it proved to be particularly weather-resistant.

Seaman's Knots:

A tight shoelace knot that does not slip open:

The Bowline Hitch results in a nonretractable Loop (in seaman's language "eye"), and is the most important knot at sea:

The Figure Eight Knot secures the end of a rope from slipping:

With the Reef Knot, you connect two equal ropes:

The Clove Hitch is used for mooring on a bollard:

SAILS

Many square yards of sailcloth are used on the equipment of a large sailing ship. The Columbia had about thirty sails of various shapes and sizes. Depending on the weather, different sets of sails were raised. The sails were heavy and were hoisted with pure muscle power via cable winches. During this strenuous work, the sailors often sang sea chanteys or seaman's songs, that facilitated toiling in a common rhythm.

In Hamburg, where today's famous entertainment district is located, there was once a working Reeperbahn, a place where ropes were made.

Windjammers

There are only a few well-to-do passengers on the *Columbia*. They travel in cabins under the quarterdeck. I watch them with curiosity but cannot find much of a difference between them and the steerage passengers.

Arend told me that big steamships are now the preferred way to travel. A ticket for a steamboat did not cost much more because those ships were able to cross the Atlantic straight across, saving time and money. I saw some of those ocean giants in the port of Bremerhaven.

When I heard that the Atlantic passage on a steamship would only take about two weeks, I was really astonished. Our trip had already taken twice as long and we haven't arrived yet. But Arend defended the *Columbia*: a true sailor lives with the winds and does not let the work of stinking, loud engines do his work!

New York is close! We're almost there. "And all in a very good time," says Arend.

HOW WERE THE STEERAGE PASSENGERS DRESSED?

Often the steerage travelers owned little more than what they were wearing, perhaps another shirt or, in addition to a pair of long trousers, a pair of shorts. The poor peasants mostly owned Sunday clothes, which were taken care of meticulously and, in the case of women's clothes, were a little more elaborate. For women traveling alone, a beautiful dress was a treasure in their search for a husband in the New World.

Land Ahoy!

At last! The seemingly endless wait is over. People dozing on the deck are jumping up and rushing to the railing. The news spreads like wildfire down to steerage, abruptly stopping all the wailing, moaning, complaining, chattering, and snickering, and leading to a hopeless confusion on the stairs. "Aaaaameeeeeerica!" Hats are flying into the air, people are cheering and screaming with joy, and some of the children are crying with excitement. They're being pushed back and forth—and can't see anything but legs and skirts—unless their fathers put them on their shoulders. Some adults are also breaking into uncontrollable tears. The relief is indescribable.

At first we see only a narrow strip of land in the distance. Gradually, the strip is broadening, and finally we can even see some buildings.

Hobgoblin

THE CITY OF NEW YORK.

The End of the Journey

We have arrived in America! It is the summer of 1872. I am one of many thousands of people who left their homes as emigrants and here at the gates of America have become immigrants in a new homeland. I carefully set foot on land. The swaying of the ship is so ingrained in my body that now the mainland seems to sway too.

Gulls are circling above us and fight screeching for a fish just seized. I follow a seagull with my eyes as it flies in a wide arc toward the open sea. I can still see the trail of white foam that the *Columbia* left in her wake. It's slowly disappearing on the horizon.

I take a deep breath, tighten the handle of my small case, and follow the other immigrants who are streaming in small groups toward a large building. As I step onto the street on the other side of the building, I almost feel like an American.

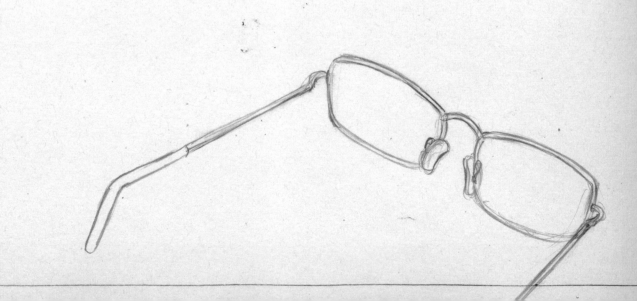

In the New World–An Outlook

When the *Columbia* reached New York as one of the last emigration sailing ships, most of the immigrants encountered few obstacles during entry. The passengers of the arriving ships, now mainly steamboats, were dispatched to Castle Garden, a warehouse in a former concert hall on the outskirts of Manhattan.

When they were no longer able to cope with the ever-swelling stream of emigrants, the immigration authorities moved operations to Ellis Island, a Manhattan island in the Hudson River, in 1892.

ELLIS ISLAND

Here the process was designed specifically to handle thousands of people every day at peak times. The entry regulations were gradually tightened, and the tests carried out on the immigrants became more and more comprehensive. In a procedure that often lasted for several days, the arriving persons had to let inspectors check them for diseases and conduct intelligence and health tests, and they had many questions to answer: What did they think they would do in the New World, were there relatives or acquaintances who expected them, how much money had they brought with them, what were their political views, had they committed a criminal offense, and much more.

Height of the Statue: 151 ft. from base to torch

Dedicated Oct 28, 1886

Give me your tired, your poor,
Your huddled masses yearning to breathe free,
The wretched refuse of your teeming shore;
Send these, the homeless, tempest-tost to me,
I lift my lamp beside the golden door!

Gebt mir eure Müden, eure Armen,
Eure geknechteten Massen,
die frei zu atmen begehren,
Die bemitleidenswerten Abgelehnten
eurer gedrängten Küsten;
Schickt sie mir, die Heimatlosen,
vom Sturme Getriebenen,
Hoch halt ich mein Licht am gold'nen Tore!

The last lines of the poem "The New Colossus"
by Emma Lazarus on the pedestal of the Statue
of Liberty

Over 12 million people immigrated to America through Ellis Island between 1892 and 1954.

RECORD YEAR:
In 1907, more than 1 million people asked for permission.

RECORD DAY:
On April 17, 1907, 11,747 immigrants arrived on Ellis Island.

Registry Hall

LOCKED GATE

It is said that about 320,000 people (2 percent of 16 million) were returned to their home countries from Ellis Island. Among them were people without means of support, the sick, the mentally ill, the disabled, the prostitutes, the illiterate, and the political radicals. Later, even entire nationalities, such as Chinese and Japanese, were excluded from entry because the Americans of European origin feared "domination by foreign elements."

Inspectors' Desks

FIRST CLASS

Well-to-do and influential immigrants were spared all this; after a short survey on board, they were taken directly to Manhattan, while the other passengers were taken by small boats from the steamship to Ellis Island.

Tools for Testing the Eyes

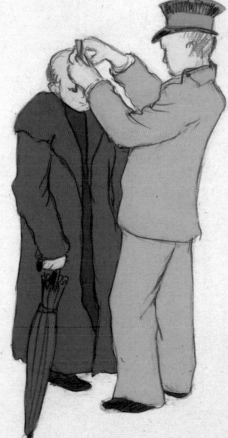

Medical Examination

In the Wild West

For most immigrants, New York was just a stopover on the way to the American West. They continued their journey on rivers and by railways. Treks of settlers, pioneers headed for undeveloped areas, moved along with packhorses and wagons.

Paddle Steamer

Caution, Crooks!

Many immigrants lost all their belongings within the first few weeks. They were easy prey for cheats. This is not surprising, for those who did not have relatives or acquaintances in the New World had to confide in strangers sooner or later, whether they were looking for a place to stay or work.

Railroad

In 2000, 42.8 million people (15 percent of the population) stated that he or she was of German (or part - German) ancestry.

Wagon

Gold Panning

THE DARK SIDE

The equality of all people emphasized in the American Declaration of Independence did not lead to equal treatment of all immigrants; nor were all persons in the United States granted equal rights. Women were not yet allowed to vote and many groups of people at that time were treated as second-class citizens.

DISAPPOINTED HOMECOMING

Awakening to American reality was often hard. There was no one who received the new arrivals with open arms. America was not a paradise. A few individuals actually gained great, abundant wealth, but many who had hoped to make quick money in America and return home after a few years with filled purses experienced defeat. Even those who had planned to live in America the rest of their lives did not all remain in the New World. The disappointment, the longing for home or for family members, was just too great.

Dear Anna,

I am glad that you are so interested in Wilhelm's story. You wanted to know how Wilhelm's life continued: He returned to Germany after six years.

Wilhelm had worked for several years in American shipyards, earing enough money to set up his own workshop at home. But he did not return to the mountains. He settled down in Hamburg. He did not want to part with the sea, the ports, and the large ships until the end of his life.

Stay safe, my dear, your Grandmother

CHRONICLE OF GERMAN EMIGRATION TO AMERICA

1607–1608 Among the pioneers who found and settle British colonies in North America are also some Germans. The first German settler is believed to be Dr. Johannes Fleischer, who arrives in 1607 with the first generation of settlers in the Jamestown Colony.

1680s German immigrants come to America in larger numbers. Their destination is the colony of Pennsylvania, whose founder, William Penn, went to Germany twice in the 1670s to promote his colony.

1683 Germantown, the first permanent German settlement, is founded in Pennsylvania by Franz Daniel Pastorius, along with thirteen families from Krefeld who belong to the religious groups of the Quakers and the Mennonites.

1708–1709 One of the most important German emigration regions is the Palatinate, which is particularly affected by wars and religious tensions. Massive emigration takes place after the harsh winter of 1708–09, when 10,000 Palatinates leave their home. By 1775, about 80,000 Palatinates have emigrated to America.

In the eighteenth century, religious minorities emigrate the most from Germany to America, including such religious groups as the Quakers, the Schwenkfelder, and the Herrnhut Brothers. Also in this century, German colonization grows, beyond Pennsylvania, to the colonies of Georgia, North Carolina, and Maine.

1816–1817 Due to the eruption of the volcano Tambora in Indonesia, one of the strongest-known volcanic eruptions ever, so much ash is thrown into the atmosphere that the Northern Hemisphere experiences extremely wet, cold summers, and the harvest of two years fails. The ensuing famine triggers a major emigration movement to America.

1830–1870 There is a wave of emigrating German Jews who do not have full citizenship rights in Bavaria and Prussia and who are also subject to discriminatory laws in other German states.

1831 Friedrich Ernst of Oldenburg becomes the first German settler in Texas, which at this time still belongs to Mexico. Between 1844 and 1847, several thousand Germans arrive in Texas when the Mainzer Adelsverein, an emigration company organized by members of the aristocracy, tries to set up a German colony there. In 1870, one-third of the inhabitants of Texas speak German. Some descendants of German-Texan immigrants still speak a dialect known as "Texas German."

1832 The Bremen Senate issues a law to protect emigrants. For example, shipping companies are required to prove the seaworthiness of their ships and to keep lists of passengers. In addition, they must now carry provisions for at least ninety days on board. This significantly reduces the mortality rate in steerage. Bremerhaven became the most important stopover for German emigrants in the second half of the nineteenth century.

1836 The first shipping line offers a regular connection between Hamburg and New York.

1848 Gold discoveries in California trigger the "gold rush" and thus create an additional incentive to emigrate.

1848–1849 After the failure of the March Revolution, a movement that demanded democracy and unification of the German states, in Germany, many democratic and liberal-minded people have to flee. They hope for a better life overseas under conditions that are politically and economically more free. Many of the "Forty-Eighters" continue their political activity in the United States.

1850–1930 Emigration becomes a mass movement.

1863 The Homestead Act becomes law. This law allows anyone over the age of twenty-one to settle on an unpopulated piece of land and seize and farm a 160-acre piece of land. After five years, the settler then becomes the owner. This law also offers an incentive to emigrate with the prospect of free land and thus economic independence.

1882 German immigration to America reaches its peak this year, with around 250,000 people.

1921–1924 The Emergency Quota Act (1921) imposes a restriction on immigration for the first time. The Immigration Act (1924) drastically restricts immigration from many countries of origin. This law stipulates that the number of immigrants allowed to arrive annually from each country to the United States is limited to 2 percent of the population that has already arrived from that country. German immigrants are preferred, however, as many Germans live in the United States by this time: 51,000 of them are allowed to enter Germany in this year.

1933 After the seizure of power by the National Socialists, many leave Germany or do not return after a stay abroad; in particular, Jewish scientists, artists, and democratic-minded politicians.

A mass entry of German asylum seekers is hampered by the American immigration law. By the beginning of the Second World War, 95,000 Austrian and German Jews are seeking refuge in the United States. The total number of Germans entering the United States from 1931 to 1940 is 114,058.

December 1945 U.S. President Harry S. Truman issues an order allowing European "displaced persons" (Jewish people, refugees, and exiles) to enter the United States under easier conditions.

1947–1949 Following World War II, many German women find a lifetime companion among the soldiers of the American occupation forces. In the period from 1947 to 1949, 13,250 German women emigrate to the United States as wives of American soldiers, and nearly 2,000 more arrive as fiancées.

1950s A total of 503,096 people emigrate to the United States, including many East Germans fleeing the Soviet occupation zone. Since then, the number of emigrants to America has dropped significantly; nevertheless, the United States remains the most popular emigration destination for Germans to this day.

1987 Green Card through the Diversity Immigrant Visa Program (DV Program)
The Diversity Immigrant Visa Program in the U.S. offers up to 50,000 immigrant visas each year. The selection is made by lottery—drawn from all entries from individuals who are from countries with low rates of immigration to the United States. The winners are entitled to live and work indefinitely in the U.S., provided they have a health certificate and can show proof of employment and housing.

Ellis Island National Museum of Immigration
(Ellis Island, NY 07305)
www.libertyellisfoundation.org/ immigration-museum
> This museum tells the story of how over 12 million immigrants entered America through Ellis Island. It is located in the former immigration station, in what is now called the Main Building.

Tenement Museum
(103 Orchard Street, New York, NY 10002)
www.tenement.org
> This museum tells the stories of immigrants who arrived in Manhattan and started new lives in the Lower East Side between the 19th and 21st centuries. Two historic tenement buildings reflect the daily lives and work of real immigrant families. Over the years, these buildings housed more than 15,000 working-class immigrants from over 20 different nations.

El Museo del Barrio
(1230 Fifth Avenue, New York, NY 10029)
www.elmuseo.org
> Located in East Harlem, this museum educates visitors about the Caribbean and Latin American experiences in the Americas.

Museum at Eldridge Street
(12 Eldridge Street, New York, NY 10002)
www.eldridgestreet.org
> This museum is located in the Lower East Side of Manhattan in the historic Eldridge Street Synagogue. The synagogue opened in 1887 as the first great house of worship in America, built by Jewish immigrants originally from Eastern Europe.

Museum of Chinese in the Americas
(215 Centre Street, New York, NY 10013)
www.mocanyc.org
> MOCA is a community organization that celebrates the immigrants who built Chinatown, the transcontinental railroad, and more.

Museum of the City of New York
(1220 Fifth Avenue, New York, NY 10029)
www.mcny.org
> Located in East Harlem, this museum recounts New York City's evolution—offering a glimpse into New York as a destination for immigrants with "then-and-now" photos and interactive kiosks and a theater.

New York Historical Society
(170 Central Park West, New York, NY 10024)
www.nyhistory.org/about
> Located on the Upper West Side, the New York Historical Society is known for being New York's first museum. Established in 1804, it offers a vast collection of art and artifacts that celebrate the important role that history plays in shaping our future. The DiMenna Children's History Museum downstairs is a small gallery that offers kids an introduction to such illustrious people as Alexander Hamilton (an immigrant from the West Indies) and Esteban Bellan (the first Latino to play pro baseball in the U.S.), as well as some of the children who boarded orphan trains or worked as newsies.

The Schomburg Center for Research in Black Culture
(515 Malcolm X Boulevard, New York, NY 10037)
www.nypl.org/locations/schomburg
> Located in Harlem, this center is one of the world's leading cultural institutions, with a rich array of events and exhibits focusing on the African American, African Diaspora, and African experiences.

German Emigration Center, Bremerhaven, Germany
(Columbusstraße 65, 27568 Bremerhaven, Germany)
www.dah-bremerhaven.de
> Embark on the journey to America! In this museum, which originated in Germany's largest emigrant harbor, you will experience the voyage from Bremerhaven to New York. What was it like to be on the ship? What happened upon arrival in the New World? What happened to the people and their descendants? These questions are answered in the information provided by the museum's replicas of the quay, the ship's decks, and Ellis Island's arrival hall.

BallinStadt Emigration Museum, Hamburg, Germany
(Veddeler Bogen 2, 20539 Hamburg, Germany)
www.ballinstadt.de
> In 1893, Albert Ballin set up a large emigration center on Hamburg's Veddel Island called the BallinStadt. At the site now is the BallinStadt Emigration Museum. In an interactive simulation, you can put yourself in the role of an emigrant. The three halls of the museum show the lives of the emigrants, the crossing of the Atlantic Ocean by ship, and finally their arrival in America.

PICTURE CREDIT

BIG THANKS FOR SUPPORT AND TRUST GOES TO ...

—My family: Max, Emma, and Matilde; Birte and Albrecht; Regina and Helle
—My studio colleagues: Uta Ratz, without whom this book would not exist in this form, and Tale Jo König
—Quint Buchholz, who accompanied me in the creation of the book
—Dagmar Schemske, who accompanied me on a journey with an unknown outcome
—Gerstenberg, my German publishing house
—Karin Heß and Jessica Fritz, who have helped me with historical questions
—Angelika C. Schmidt-Lange, for the translation and for the joint Texan reading tour that showed me
  the great interest students have in the history of European immigration to America; big thanks also
  to Wolfgang Schmidt, Andrew Rushton, Beth Terrill, and NorthSouth Books for the joint adventure
  of bringing Wilhelm to America
—All those who contributed to *Wilhelm's Journey* in various ways
—All those who supported me during busy work times

Thank you to the German Emigration Center in Bremerhaven for providing comprehensive insight into the topic of historical emigration and for the experiences I was able to gather from visiting youngsters in the Children's Museum of the DAH, the Maritime Museum Unterweser, and the German Maritime Museum in Bremerhaven.

The Columbia is one of the last large sailing ships that brought emigrants from Bremerhaven to New York.